little Chippy

LAUREN DOUGLAS

ILLUSTRATIONS BY QBN Studios

Brooklyn Writers Press
Brooklyn, NY
www.brooklynwriterspress.com

978-1-952991-10-3 e-Book ISBN
978-1-952991-11-0 Paperback ISBN
978-1-952991-12-7 Hardback ISBN

LCCN: 2021910560

Dedicated to all of my furry family members and those with feathers and scales, who enrich my life and give me joy every single day. Past, present, and future. Thank you to Chippy for loving me at first "bite".

This is a heartwarming tale about exploring new places. About a little dog named Chippy who gets over any challenge he faces.

When Chippy was a pup, he lived upstate.
He would play under the sun, in the
grass, and behind his home's gate.

Running and playing brought him so much joy, especially when he got a brand-new toy.

Being outside brought him delight.
The wind blowing in his fur
made Chippy feel just right.

Then one day, he moved to the city,
which seemed so far.
Chippy had to travel a long
way in a very big car.

The skyscrapers were giant and gave him a new view, but after a while, Chippy knew, it just wouldn't do.

The big city was too loud
and way too crowded.

He couldn't make friends
because everyone SHOUTED!
Around so many people,
Chippy was shy.

And he also missed swimming, which made him cry.

Then on a train, he went in
search of a pool and a yard.
And to make new friends, which
he hoped wouldn't be too hard.

Little Chippy found a new home
where he could play all day.
He was happy to move to
a place right by the bay.

The only thing was,
meeting new dogs made Chippy wary.
Making new friends can sometimes be scary.

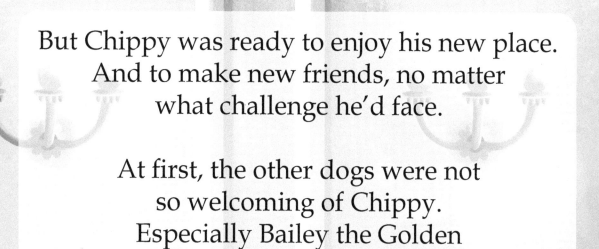

But Chippy was ready to enjoy his new place.
And to make new friends, no matter
what challenge he'd face.

At first, the other dogs were not
so welcoming of Chippy.
Especially Bailey the Golden
who could be quite snippy.

But Chippy brought treats
and toys to share.
He showed the others he was kind
and would always play fair.

Coco the Brussel gave the
other dogs advice.
She woofed, they should all
"try to be extra nice."

And Reggie the Yorkie made
a super-smart request.
Reggie arfed, "Be fair to all.
That is always what's best."

The other dogs finally let him
play with them in the park.
Together they chased big birds, and
Chippy let out the most cheerful bark.

Soon Chippy became part of the pack.
With his new friends, he would
swim, play, and even enjoy a snack.

And like all friends, they would sometimes fight, but they always made up and would quickly unite.

When nightfall would come, they all cuddled together. Chippy and his new friends became a family forever.

ABOUT THE AUTHOR

Lauren Douglas has had dogs all of her life with her family currently having 9! Little Chippy is a true story about Chippy living with her while she lived in upstate New York and then moving to New York City. He eventually became part of her parent's pack of dogs on Long Island by the Bay; where Chippy now happily and swimmingly resides. Having Grown up in a true melting pot, Lauren felt Chippy's adventures paralleled her life and she felt it was important to spread the message of adapting to change whether it be a new home or new friends. In her free time, Lauren loves to read, dabble in arts & crafts, and to pester her 2 younger brothers. Most importantly, Lauren loves to play and cuddle with all her dogs!

ABOUT THE ILLUSTRATOR

QBN Studios is a small Illustration Studio located in Vernon Connecticut. Owners Quynh Nguyen and Christopher MacCoy are passionate about helping Authors fulfill their dreams and bring their words to life. QBN Studio's goal is to create an immersive experience for their audiences to tumble headfirst into imaginary worlds. Follow us on Instagram @qbnstudios for the latest updates on illustrations, books, and other projects.

Thank You for Reading
Little Chippy

If you enjoyed this book, please consider leaving a short review
on Goodreads or your website of choice.

Reviews help both readers and writers. They are an easy way to support
good work and help to encourage the continued release of quality content.

Connect with Lauren Douglas
littlechippybook.com

Want the latest from the Brooklyn Writers Press?
Browse our complete catalog
brooklynwriterspress.com

CPSIA information can be obtained
at www.ICGtesting.com
Printed in the USA
BVHW021952050222
627839BV00002B/14

* 9 7 8 1 9 5 2 9 9 1 1 1 0 *